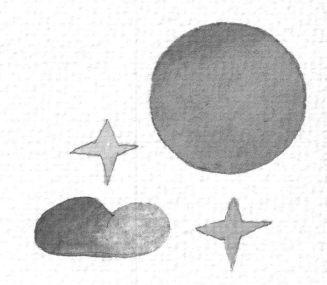

For Elena

"You human child, you are also a star who is always expanding your circle." —H. F. Micheelsen

By Geraldine Elschner

Moonchild,
Star of the Sea

Illustrated by Lieselotte Schwarz

Translated by J. Alison James

A Michael Neugebauer Book

NORTH-SOUTH BOOKS
New York · London

A little star sat on a silver moonbeam and gazed down at the earth.

"What are those dark places?" the star asked the moon.

"That is the land, where people live," she answered.

"What are those lovely blue places?"

"That is the sea," said the moon. "We are good friends."

"Please, tell me more about the sea," begged the little star.

"The sea is wonderful," said the moon. "Every night it glimmers with light from me; every day it sparkles in the sun. The sea is blue when the sky is laughing and gray when the sky is sad. Sometimes the sea is green like the algae, sometimes white like the clouds. The sea is full of magic."

The little star couldn't hear enough about the sea.

"Dear moon, I want to go there and see it myself," the little star said one day.

The moon smiled at him. "For every star there is a time when they want to go to earth," the moon said quietly. "Now it is your turn. You will lose your lightshirt and put on a seashirt. You will become a sea star. You will live on the earth until you have learned all you can learn, and then you will return here to the sky. It will be a wonderful journey."

The moon looked fondly at the little star. "I will wait here for you," she said. "But everywhere and always my light will keep you company, even when you cannot see it."

So the star shut his eyes
and a great beam of light
shone out of the sky
and into the night
of the deep, deep sea.

The star slept deeply for a long time. When he woke,
he felt the stroke of the water on his arms. He stretched.
"Look, he's moving," whispered a voice near him.
"How beautiful he is," said another.
The sea flowers greeted him with open blossoms.

And so began a new life for the little star.
He played every day with his friends and danced in the waves of
the sea. He swam with schools of fish through forests of seaweed
and caves of coral. Down in the deep water all was still; at the
surface the waves swished and swelled. The little star was thrilled.

Each night he made his way back to a cliff that rose up from the
beach. Here he felt safe. The moon smiled at him from her place
in the sky. He waved to her and told her what he had learned that
day. Even if she couldn't hear, he knew she understood.

But one day there wasn't much to tell. He had learned all he could in his beloved place near the cliff, so the sea star swam away. He longed to see distant shores, far-off oceans, and unimaginable creatures.

What a journey! Nervously he watched the bright bustle of a port city—ships and people, lights and music.

He swam on the surface and followed the scent of wild and strange flowers. He floated past islands bursting with green. He listened to voices cawing and cooing, hooting and mooing, and singing songs. Then the sea star went under the sea. He swam with a whale as large as a ship through deep ocean canyons and towering cliffs. He learned from the dolphins to surf the waves and to dive when the ocean was surging with storms.

The little star journeyed through the sea from land to land throughout the world.

In the south, he met children playing in the sand.

In the north, he saw houses blanketed with snow.

Just like the sea, the land was full of magic, and each day the sea star learned something new.

Time passed, days and nights, years and years. The little star grew tired. One evening he heard a sweet sound—the song of a nightingale—that he had never heard before. He felt a rush of thanks in his heart, for he had not heard anything new for a very long time. That was when he knew that he had learned all he could.

So the star decided to go back home. He returned to the sea and
swam back to his beloved cliff. What a joy to see his friends again!
He told them stories about all the things he had seen all over the
world. They told him stories of what had happened there in the bay.

Then it was time—
On a lovely autumn night, when the moon was full and his
friends were all around . . .

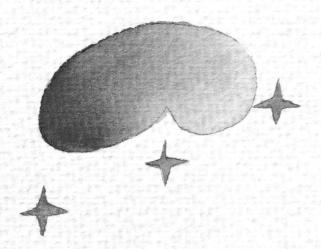

The star shut his eyes
and a great beam of light
shone out of the sea
and into the night
of the deep, deep sky.

The star woke to the wind brushing his arms. He felt as if he'd
slept deep and long.
The moon smiled at him. "Hello again, dear star," she said.
"How nice to have you back."

And far away on a lonely beach, a child found a star washed
up on the sand—and carried it home, a treasure in hand.

Copyright © 2002 by Michael Neugebauer Verlag, an imprint of Nord-Süd Verlag AG, Gossau Zürich, Switzerland
First published in Switzerland under the title *Sternenkind*. English translation copyright © 2002 by North-South Books Inc., New York

First published in the United States, Great Britain, Canada, Australia, and New Zealand in 2002 by North-South Books,
an imprint of Nord-Süd Verlag AG, Gossau Zürich, Switzerland.

Distributed in the United States by North-South Books Inc., New York.

Library of Congress Cataloging-in-Publication Data is available.
A CIP catalogue record for this book is available from The British Library.
ISBN 0-7358-1664-6 (trade edition) 10 9 8 7 6 5 4 3 2 1
ISBN 0-7358-1665-4 (library edition) 10 9 8 7 6 5 4 3 2 1
Printed in Italy

For more information about our books, and the authors and artists who create them, visit our web site: www.northsouth.com